PATRICK'S DREAM

Told and Illustrated by

Cynthia *and* William BIRRER

WALKER BOOKS
LONDON

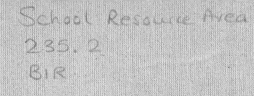

For Olga

First published 1989 by
Julia MacRae Books
This edition published 1991 by
Walker Books Ltd, 87 Vauxhall Walk
London SE11 5HJ

© 1989 Cynthia and William Birrer

Printed and bound in Hong Kong by
Sheck Wah Tong Printing Press Ltd

British Library Cataloguing in Publication Data
Birrer, Cynthia
Patrick's dream.
1. Christian church. Patrick, Saint –
Biographies
I. Title   II. Birrer, William
270.2'092'4
ISBN 0-7445-2006-1

Patrick was born in Roman Britain, the son of a centurion. The kings of Ireland often raided the west of Britain and in one of these raids the young boy was carried across the sea into slavery.

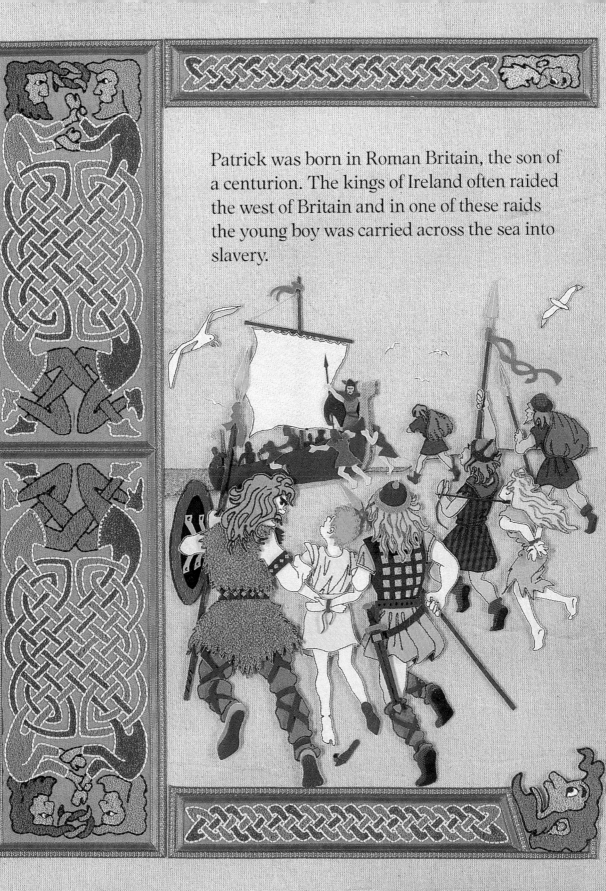

Seven long years later Patrick escaped to a
harbour where traders were trying in vain to load
a cargo of wild Irish wolfhounds. As he
approached the animals fell quiet. The captain
looked at Patrick in amazement. "Please join our
crew," he begged.

During the voyage a storm drove the ship ashore. Wandering for days through dry and barren land, the men became weak with hunger. As Patrick knelt and prayed, a herd of swine appeared, and the famine was broken.

At home at last, Patrick studied hard and became a priest. And then one night, in a dream, he heard the voice of the Irish people: "We ask thee, holy youth, come and walk among us once more."

So Patrick set out for Ireland, where he dedicated himself as a bishop to spending the rest of his days winning the people to Christ.

In spring he journeyed to Tara. The High King of Tara was warned by his Druids that Patrick was a threat to his heathen kingdom, but he laughed scornfully at all the tales he heard. Such a meek and gentle man could not be a threat to him.

The King prepared to light the first fire of spring to proclaim the rebirth of the sun after winter's death, but Patrick lit another nearby to celebrate the resurrection of the Son of God. "What do I see yonder?" roared the King. "Who dares to light a fire before me?"

"If that fire is not quenched this day it will burn forever," his Druids told him. "Moreover, it will overcome all the fires of our religion." The King and his men sped across the plain in their chariots but they stopped when they reached the circle of flames.

"Slay him!" commanded the King. At this, Patrick cried
aloud and instantly lightning struck all about, an icy

wind blew, and a great earthquake shook the ground,
scattering chariot, horse, and man alike.

By now, the King was alarmed. He invited Patrick to Tara. Further along the way he hid, intending to kill the holy man and his company as they passed. But Patrick and his followers took on the shapes of leaping deer and escaped unharmed.

The King returned to Tara to host the feast in the
Great Hall. The doors were barred, but it seemed
nothing could stop Patrick, who calmly appeared
to sit beside the King.

The Druids were now fearful and began to chant. As their voices swelled, snow fell upon the sun-drenched fields. Challenged to stop the falling flakes, Patrick lifted his crozier skywards. The snow vanished and the sun glowed again in the heavens.

Then the Druids built a house, partly of green wood and partly of dry. The Chief Druid entered the green side while Patrick's disciple entered the other, and the house was put to the torch.

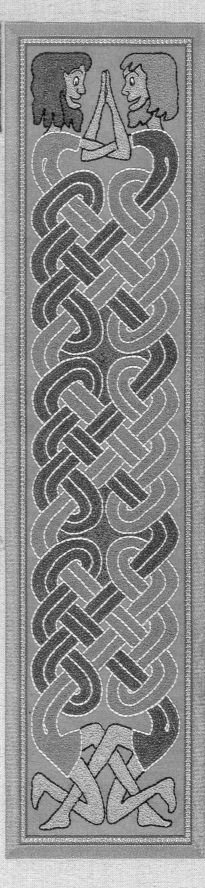

Instantly the greenery burst into flames, hurling the Druid skywards. The dry part would not burn and its occupant emerged untouched.

The defeated Druids listened as Patrick spoke sternly of the one God who is also Three. "Here on the single stem of the shamrock are three leaves which together form a perfect whole. So it is with the Trinity."

Although the High King remained forever pagan, from that day he allowed Patrick to spread the Gospel of Christ far and wide throughout Ireland.

Until, grown old but little meeker,
He took his final rest.
And tales of his renown
Are woven into tapestries
That reach from town to town.